FOREWORD

DRAMASCRIPTS are intended for use in secondary schools, amateur theatrical groups and youth clubs. The plays range widely from established classics to new works and adaptations of books and film scripts. They may be used in a variety of ways: read privately for pleasure or aloud in groups, acted in the classroom, church hall or youth club, or in public performance.

It is not easy to find contemporary plays for young people to read or perform which will both entertain and challenge them. Robert Westall's story THE MACHINE-GUNNERS has been extremely popular with pupils for many years. The young are perceptive critics, and they respond to its realism, humour and truthfulness. Through the adventures and experiences of Chas McGill and his gang we follow a group of young people caught in the middle of a 'grown-ups' war, and as they play out their fantasies they are forced to come to terms with the human meaning of that war. This skilful adaptation of Mr Westall's novel is certain to become a greatly valued addition to the DRAMASCRIPTS series.

GUY WILLIAMS
Advisory Editor

PRODUCTION NOTES

It is possible for music to play an important part in a performance of this adaptation of THE MACHINE-GUNNERS. In the original production, a school orchestra played, before the performance began, a selection of ballroom melodies of the 1940s, and couples in service uniforms of the time danced over the acting area and through the auditorium before the start of the opening air raid. The musical themes were repeated, then, throughout the performance either to create a mood, to facilitate a change of scene, or to suggest the passage of time.

It would be difficult to perform THE MACHINE-GUNNERS convincingly without exciting lighting and sound effects that will transport the members of the audience back, in their imaginations, to the desperate days (and nights) of the Second World War. Fortunately, sound effects can be edited, as required, from the many excellent recorded anthologies available. These can then be played through any standard sound system at appropriate moments in the play.

In adapting the novel for the stage, the numerous locations have had to be somewhat condensed. A possible arrangement of the acting area has been provided opposite. This may help producers — and members of the audience — to identify the key locations, many of which can be 'doubled' in the course of the play.

The play was first performed by pupils of Colfox School, Bridport.

A POSSIBLE ARRANGEMENT OF THE ACTING AREA

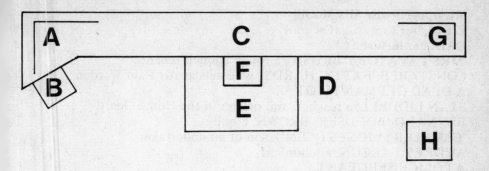

AUDIENCE

A The McGill kitchen
B The McGill air raid shelter
C Street area
D Street area
E School playground;
   Classroom;
   NICKY's garden;
   Near the sea
F THE GANG's fortress
G The home of GRAND-DA and NANA McGILL, and bombed and
   damaged houses
H The wood with the crashed German plane; the Home Guard
   Command Post

THE CHARACTERS

MUM, otherwise Mrs McGill
CHAS, her son, still at school
DAD, her husband
'MRS LAVATORY BRUSH', a rough council tenant
CONSTABLE 'FATTY' HARDY, who acts as Air Raid Warden
A DEAD GERMAN PILOT
STAN LIDDELL, a teacher, and officer in the Home Guard
BERNARD 'BODDSER' BROWN, a bully
'CEMETERY' JONES ('CEM'), son of an undertaker
AUDREY PARTON, a schoolgirl
A POLICE SERGEANT
MRS SPALDING, a neighbour of the McGills
COLIN, Mrs Spalding's son
A POLICEMAN
NANA McGILL, Chas' grandmother
GRAND-DA McGILL, Chas' grandfather
'CLOGGER' DUNCAN, a boy from Glasgow
'NICKY' NICHOL, only son of a war-widow
NICKY'S MOTHER
NICKY'S MOTHER'S BOYFRIEND (in charge of naval ratings)
'CARROTS', a member of Chas' gang
DUTY OFFICER 'SANDY' SANDERSON, of the Home Guard
RUDI GERLATH, a German rear-gunner
A WOMAN IN A DAMAGED HOUSE
HER BEDRIDDEN MOTHER
MRS FLYNN, a stout woman
MISS SMITH, thin and prim
MRS BROWN, Boddser's mother
SERGEANT MULLINS
MR WHITELOAD, a member of the Home Guard
MAJOR KOSLOWSKI of the Polish Free Army

CHILDREN, STRETCHER BEARERS, CHAIN-GANG WORKERS,
MEMBERS OF THE HOME GUARD, MEMBERS OF THE POLISH
FREE ARMY, NURSES, etc.

SCENE 1

(The **McGill** *kitchen, after an air raid. It is early morning.* **Mum** *is there.)*

Mum *(Calling).* Chas!

*(***Chas** *emerges from the shelter. He looks round carefully and then enters the kitchen.* **Mum** *calls again.)*

. . . Father!

*(***Dad** *enters wearily and sits down)*

Dad. You remember that lass in the greengrocer's?

Mum. The ginger-haired one?

Dad. Uh-huh. A direct hit. They found half of her in the front garden and the other half right across the road.

Mum *(Fighting emotion).* She didn't believe in shelters. She was always frightened of being buried alive.

Dad *(To Chas).* Your rabbits are all right. Chinny had some glass in her hutch, but I shifted it. There's six panes out in the greenhouse. If it goes on this way, there'll be no chrysanths for Christmas.

Mum *(Shaking slightly).* It won't be the same without chrysanths. . .*(To* **Chas***).* . . Here's your breakfast. . .*(As* **Chas** *eats quietly, listening to the conversation,* **Mum** *goes on).* . . I thought we were a goner last night, I really did. That dive-bomber. . . Thought it was going to land on top of the shelter. . . Mrs Spalding had one of her turns.

Dad. It wasn't a dive-bomber. It had two engines. RAF lads after him, right on his tail. That's why he came so low. But they got him. Crashed on the old laundry. Full bomb-load. I felt the heat on my face a mile away. . . *(Seeing* **Mum's** *reaction, he says).* . . Nobody killed, Love, been empty for years.

Chas. Can I go and see it?

Dad. You can go and look. . . But you'll find nothing but bricks.

Mum. Do you think he should?

Dad. Let him go. There's nothing left.

Mum. No unexploded bombs?

Dad. No. A quiet night, really. Lots of our fighters up.

Chas. Can I borrow your old shopping basket?

Mum. I suppose so. But don't lose it. And none of your old rubbish in the house. Take it straight to the greenhouse.

Dad. What time is school?

Chas. Half-past ten. . . *(Cheekily).* . . The raid went on past midnight.

1

SCENE 2

(In a street, the morning after the raid. People dig; chain-gangs shift bricks, etc. **Chas** *walks along, searching. He finds the tail-fin of an incendiary bomb and bits of an aluminium plane. Then he comes to a council house. The windows are missing; the ceiling is down; and the door is hanging loose.* **The Tenant** — *a rough lady known locally as* **'Mrs Lavatory Brush'** — *and* **Her Children** *are salvaging their belongings.)*

Tenant *(To Chas).* You can stop staring. Ghoul! Haven't you anything better to do?

Chas. Can I see the engine?

Tenant. No. It's ours.

Chas. No, it isn't. It belongs to the Air Ministry. By law!

Tenant. No, it don't. It's ours, 'cos it knocked our 'ouse down. Get lost, or I'll set Cuthbert on you.

> *(***The Children*** *look threatening)*

Chas. You're all rubbish.

Tenant. Go back where you belong. 'S our engine. The newspaper's coming to take photos today.

> *(She adjusts a segment of front door. It is marked 'BUSNES AS USUAL'.* **A Child** *heaves a stone.* **Chas** *runs.)*

SCENE 3

(In a bombed street, **'Fatty' Hardy,** *an Air Raid Warden, is guarding an engine. A large propeller sticks out from under a tarpaulin.* **Chas** *walks up, eyes the engine enviously, and wonders how he can get rid of* **Hardy.***)*

Chas *(Pretending to cry, in panic, and raising his hand, as at school).* Please, Sir, Mum says 'Come, quick!' There's a deep hole in our garden and something ticking in it!. . .

> *(There is a pause.* **Hardy** *is worried, and in a dilemma.* **Chas** *presses on.)*

. . . Hurry, Sir! There's little kids all round it, looking down the hole!

2

Hardy *(Grabbing* **Chas** *by the shoulders).* Where? Where? Take me! Take me!

Chas. Please, Sir, no, Sir. Mum says I mustn't go back there in case it goes off. I've got to go to me Gran's, Sir. The bomb's at 19, Marston Road.

Hardy *(Running towards Marston Road).* Don't touch the engine!

*(***Chas** *starts to pull and bash at the propeller, but he fails to move it)*

Chas *(In frustration).* Nazi pigs!

Hardy *(Coming back).* Oi! You!

*(***Chas** *runs away.)*

SCENE 4

(By a wrecked plane, in a wood. It is dark, and flies are buzzing. **Chas**, *with a torch, approaches the plane.* **Hardy** *can be heard shouting in the distance.)*

Chas *(To himself, but aloud, as he finds the tailplane).*

Flippin' 'eck! It's a plane! That's a turn-up!. . . *(He assumes the voice of a BBC announcer.).* . . 'The mystery bomber shot down over Garmouth on the night of the First of November has been identified as a new and secret variation of the Heinkel H.E. 3. It was found by a nearly unknown schoolboy, Charles McGill of Garmouth High School. . . Sorry, I'll read that again. . . Of Form 3A at Garmouth High School. There is no doubt that but for the sharp eyes of this young man, several enemy secret weapons vital to the Blitzkrieg would have remained undiscovered'. . . *(He speaks again in his own voice).* . . Eh? Ssh!. . .

(He sees a machine gun. He tugs at it. **The Dead Gunner** *flops forward out of the undergrowth.* **Chas**, *terrified but fascinated, reaches out to touch* **The Gunner**, *whose arm and hand are quite stiff. Flies are buzzing.* **Chas** *pukes. A factory hooter sounds.* **Chas** *hurries away.)*

3

SCENE 5

(The McGill *kitchen.* Mum *is there as* Chas *enters.)*

Mum. Looks like you seen a ghost! What have you been up to?

Chas. Nothing, Mum. Been running 'cos I was late. I got the stitch.

Mum. Where's my basket?

Chas. I forgot it. It's all right. I've hidden it safe. Get it tonight after school.

Mum. See you do. Your Dad bought me that when we were courting. Now, off to school before you get the stick.

*(*Chas *hurries out)*

SCENE 6

(A schoolroom. Liddell *is teaching a class that includes* 'Boddser' Brown *and* 'Cem' Jones. Chas *enters, late. He sits, but he is restless and cannot settle to work.)*

Liddell *(To* Chas*).* What's the matter with you this morning, McGill? You ill?

Chas *(Thinking quickly).* Sorry, Sir. Couldn't sleep in the shelter. Woman next door had kittens because she thought the bomber was diving on her personally.

*(*The Class *roars with laughter)*

Liddell *(Quietly).* Fool!

Chas *(Secretively, to* Cem, *while* Liddell *patrols).* I've found something. It's big. I'll need your cart to shift it.

Cem. Can't. Got my Guy on it.

Chas. What d'you want a Guy for? No bonfires allowed this year. No fireworks in the shops. Nothing. You're potty.

Cem. I use the money I collect to buy sweets.

Chas. Look, this is *big*. . . bigger than anything you've ever seen.

Cem. Go on! You always say that!

Chas. Come and see for yourself, then.

Cem. When?

Chas. Tonight.

Cem. Got to do me homework before the raid starts. We've only got one candle in the shelter.

4

Chas. Look, I'll give you an incendiary bomb fin. A real smasher. Not a dent. . .

Cem. I'll come for the fin, then. But I don't believe the other.

Chas *(Having a brainwave).* And bring your cart with the Guy still on it. . .

Liddell *(Sharply).* McGill!

Chas. Sorry Sir.

SCENE 7

(Out of doors, at night. **Chas** *and* **Cem** *are pulling a cart.* **Audrey Parton** *approaches.)*

Chas and Cem. Oh, hell!

Audrey. Where are you kids going?

Chas *(Disgusted).* Ha! Ha! Faff off, Audrey Parton. We're busy.

Audrey. Busy? Little things please little minds.

Chas. While greater fools look on. . .

Audrey. In disgust. . .

Cem. At themselves. . .

(There is a pause. Stalemate has been reached.)

Audrey. Where are you going? Can I come?

(The Boys confer)

Chas and Cem. All right. You can come with us.

(The Three move off)

Audrey *(Loudly).* And I'm not doing any dirty things with you two in this wood, so you needn't think I am. I don't mind kissing, but no more.

Cem. E-E-urk! Who'd want to, with you?

Chas. Ssh! . . . *(As they reach the wrecked bomber).* . . There's a dead German inside. You can look if you want, Cem, but not Audrey. Girls can't stand it.

Cem. My Dad'll see to what's left of him.

Chas. They won't bury him here.

Audrey. Poor man! He's a long way from home!

Chas. Look! We came for this. . .

5

*(He waggles the machine gun. Then, **The Boys** set to work sawing, while **Audrey** holds the torch.)*

Audrey. There's a funny smell. . .

Cem. That's him. It gets worse as it goes on.

Audrey. I want to go home.

Cem. Keep that torch straight!. . . *(In disgust)*. . . Blooming girls!

Audrey. Oh, shut up!

Hardy *(In the distance.)* Put that light out!

Cem. God! It's the Warden!

> *(A police whistle sounds. There is a burst of fire from the machine gun.)*

Cem. Let's run! What're we gonna do?

Chas. Where's your Guy? Come on! Down his leg with it!

> *(**The Boys** get busy hiding the gun)*

Audrey. Come on! Come on!

Chas. Let's go. . .

> *(The air-raid warning siren sounds)*

Audrey *(Terrified).* Oh, no! What shall we do?

Chas. It's just what we need. I'm getting this home while the streets are empty. Audrey! On your bike and get to a shelter!

> *(**Audrey** hurries away.)*

Cem. We'll go the back way. Come on!

> *(There are plane sounds, flashes and distant explosions. **Chas** and **Cem** can be seen in relief by the light of the flashes.)*

Chas. It's a sneak raider. . .

Cem. More than one. Half a dozen. . .

Chas. They're dropping parachute flares. . .

> *(**The Boys** hear the sound of anti-aircraft guns)*

Chas *(Shouting).* Go on! Get the bastards! Kill the bastards!
(They hurry away.)

SCENE 8

*(The **McGill** kitchen. Dad is there as Chas enters, leaving Cem at the door.)*

Dad. Where the hell have you been? Your mother's worried sick. Who's that with you?

Chas. Cem.

Dad. Get down the shelter, both of you. I'll tell his mother he's all right.

Chas. What about the Guy?

Dad. He's used to it. Now, in!

(The Boys go to the shelter)

SCENE 9

(In the garden, outside The McGills' shelter. It is very early in the morning. The 'All Clear' siren sounds. Carrying a towel, Chas creeps out of the shelter and goes to Cem's Guy. He takes out the gun, wraps the towel round it, and hides it in some convenient place.)

Dad *(Calling from the shelter).* You pulling Cem's Guy to bits?

Chas. Just mending the leg. . .

Dad. Mending it? It weighs a ton. Anyway, you leave that to Cem. It's his Guy. I sometimes think you're a bit too free with other people's property. No sense of 'Mine' and 'Thine', that's your trouble.

Chas. Yes. Dad.

(Dad straightens a chrysanthemum and goes into the house)

SCENE 10

(In the school playground, in daytime. Boys and Girls are playing in groups. Chas and Boddser meet, stare at each other, and pass on. Then Cem approaches Chas.)

Cem. Chas! Eh, you know them round things full of bullets? Got four more. They were clipped to the fuselage near the gunner's feet.

Chas *(Trying to keep his secret from Boddser and His Gang).* Where you got them?

Cem. In my Dad's potting shed. 'S all right. He never goes there since the war. It's all cobwebs.

Chas. Is the gunner still there?

Cem. Yeah. Phew! He don't half niff.

Chas. I don't know how you can stand it. Ain't you got no feelings?

7

Cem. We get used to it. When my Dad was on an embalming course he saw one fellah eating his sandwiches, reading a book propped against a body.

Chas. E-E-urk!. . .

(They cross to where **A Laughing Group** *surrounds* **Boddser**, *and* **Chas** *says)*

. . . Hey! What's up?

Boddser. Hah! McGill, king of the incendiary bombs!

Chas. Why don't you stick that nose cone where it belongs? It would just go with your glasses.

Boddser. Got something better than that. Look!

(He dangles a flying helmet under Chas' nose)

Cem *(Warning)*. Watch yourself, now, Chas.

Chas *(To* **Boddser***)*. Where'd you get that? Woolworths?

Boddser. Never you mind. That's genuine Nazi, and so's this money. And what about this?. . . *(He shows a photograph, and says)*. . . 'Mein Liebling', she's called.

Chas *(Feeling sick)*. You. . .

Cem *(Interrupting swiftly)*. Come on, Chas!

(He pulls **Chas** *away)*

Chas. He's disgusting. You know what he's been doing?

Boddser *(Shouting)*. That's better than your rotten shrapnel, any day!

SCENE 11

(The schoolroom. **The Class** *sits, waiting.* **Cem** *comes in. He is out of breath.)*

Audrey *(To* **Chas***)*. They've found it.

Chas. The police?

Audrey. Yes. Watch out! Tell you later.

Liddell *(Holding up the tail-fin of an incendiary bomb)*. Found this, this morning.

A Member of the Class. That's nothing, Sir. Boddser Brown's got fifteen and McGill's got ten.

Liddell. Not like this one. It's a new type the Jerries have just started to use. Twice as powerful. In fact, they've started using a whole range of new weapons. I don't suppose any of you will take the

8

blindest bit of notice of what I say, but you should all be extra-vigilant when you are out and about. . . *(He holds up a photograph and says)* . . . Now I just want to. . .

Chas *(Tipping ink over **Cem**'s trousers).* Oh, hell!. . .

*(The attention of **The Class** is distracted from **Liddell**. **Chas** says to **Cem***)

. . . That's a picture of our gun he's got! Watch your face!. . .

*(To **Liddell***). . . Sorry, Sir. Spilt it, Sir.

Liddell. For Heaven's sake, McGill, will you pay attention? And you, Jones. This is a picture of a German aircraft machine-gun. The MG 15, calibre 7.62 millimetres, firing one thousand rounds a minute, effective range one mile. . .

*(There is no response from **The Class** so **Liddell** says)*

. . . Right! Open your English exercise books! I want an essay on 'War Souvenirs'.

Chas *(Reading aloud as he writes).* 'I used to have the best collection of war souvenirs in this town. I have eleven incendiary-bomb fins, twenty-six spent bullets, eighteen pieces of shrapnel, including one piece a foot long, and fifty empty cartridge cases.

'But my collection is now second-best because Boddser Brown in 3B has beaten me. He has a 3.7 inch nose-cone, and a pongy German flier's helmet, and lots of German money with Hitler's face on it, and a picture of a German girl in pigtails called "Mein Liebling". I wish I knew how he got these things 'cos he's beating me hollow and if I can't beat him soon, I shall have to give up and start collecting cigarette cards instead. . . '

Liddell. Right! Pass your books in!

*(**Chas** gives **Cem** a 'thumbs-up' sign)*

Chas. Come on!

Cem. Where?

Chas. We've got to hide that gun. Fast!

(They sneak out)

SCENE 12

*(In the garden, outside **The McGills'** shelter. **Chas** and **Cem** come and move the gun. **Cem** takes it away.)*

9

SCENE 13

(The McGill *kitchen.* **The Police** *and* **Liddell** *are interviewing* **Chas** *and*
Cem. Dad *and* **Mum** *are present.)*

Sergeant. You are Charles Harold McGill?
Dad. No. He's Charlie Chan the burglar.
Liddell. Let's get to business, may we?
Sergeant. Charles McGill, have you found any. . . war souvenirs in the
    last few days?
Chas. Only a tail-fin, but I'm swapping that with Cem.
Sergeant. Are you sure that's all?
Chas. Yeah.
Sergeant. You were down West Chirton, the morning after that bomber
    crashed. Why are you looking so guilty, Lad?
Chas. I tried to pinch a propeller off an engine. The Warden chased me.
Sergeant. Where do you keep your souvenirs?
Chas. In Dad's shed. By the shelter.
Sergeant. Let's go and see, shall we?. . .

> *(They go and rummage around.* **The Sergeant** *finds a cache of*
> *cartridge cases. He says)*

. . . I think these better come along with us.
Chas. But they're mine! I've been collecting all year!
Sergeant. The nation needs scrap metal.
Chas. They're the second-best collection in Garmouth!
Dad. Let the lad keep them, Sergeant.
Sergeant. All such things are the property of the Crown.
Dad. Tripe! Just like a copper.
Sergeant. Take him away, please, Sir. We'll search your whole house
    and garden, if need be.
Dad *(To* **Mum***).* Put him to bed, Mother. I'm staying here. You can't
    trust coppers. . . *(To* **The Sergeant***).* . . And you mind my plants!
Sergeant. Be sure to let us know if anything turns up, Sir.
Dad. Get lost! I'll have the lawyers on you in the morning.

SCENE 14

(The McGill *kitchen and shelter, later.* **Mum** *is cooking.* **Chas** *is reading.*
Dad *comes back from work.)*

Dad *(To* **Mum***).* Hello, Love.

Mum. Here's your supper, nice and hot. . .

(As **Dad** *washes his hands, she says)*

. . . Nice having the raid early for once. I could do with a good night's sleep in me own bed.

Dad. Don't count your chickens. There's still a 'Yellow Alert' on. I think I'd better get me uniform on.

Mum. Your tea will be spoiled.

Dad. Put it back in the oven. . .

(The lights go out. Plane engines are heard. Flashes and explosions follow. Guns are fired.)

Mum *(With a scream).* Oh! Those lovely sausages!

Dad. Get down, both of you! Away from the window! Now, run for it!

(They scramble to the shelter and land in a heap)

Mum *(Lighting an oil lamp).* Did you shut the door, Love? Someone might nip in and steal the insurance policies. And where's Mrs Spalding and Colin?

(More plane noises)

Dad. The brutes is coming again! Where's the guns? Where's the fighters?

(With a screech, **Mrs Spalding** *crashes into the shelter. She is followed by her son* **Colin.***)*

Mum. Oh! Is she dead?

Dad. No, but she's got her knickers round her ankles!

Mrs Spalding. I had to hop all the way. I was on the outside lav, and couldn't finish. The blast took the lav. door off and they've hit the Rex cinema as well. Is there a spot of brandy?

Colin. I pulled the chain, Mum. It flushed all right.

Chas. You'll get the VC for that.

Mum *(To* **Chas***).* Shut up! Have you no feelings?

(As those in the shelter listen to the sounds outside, **Chas,** *lost in a fantasy world, stands up, holding the gun and firing at the enemy. He scores a direct hit each time.)*

Dad. Chas! Come on! Get to sleep!

11

SCENE 15

(Outside **The McGills'** *shelter, next morning.* **The Family** *emerges.)*

Dad. Chas, Lad, I'm going to see If Nana and Grand-da are all right. Most of the bombs fell by the river last night. I want you to come with me.

Mum. Don't take him, Jack.

Dad. He's going. He's near fifteen, now. And there'll be errands to run. Clearing to do.

Mum. He'd better wear his best suit, then.

Dad. Don't be daft, Woman. It's not a funeral yet. . . *(To Chas). . .* Come on, Son.

SCENE 16

(Down town. There are stretcher-bearers, chain-gang workers, etc. By a road block, **Dad** *and* **Chas** *meet* **A Policeman.***)*

Dad. Can you tell us which roads are open, down town?

Policeman *(Busy).* I can't. You'll have to ask further on.

*(***Dad** *and* **Chas** *pass* **Families Clearing Rubble***)*

Dad. We'll knock at the front door. Stand beside me, and if I say 'Shut your eyes', you shut them bloody quick. Understand?

*(***Nana** *appears)*

Nana. I knew you'd come! And the boy! Look at the roof. D'you see what them Germans has done? If I could get hold of that bloody Hilter, I'd strangle him, the snotty-nosed git. He's really done for Grand-da, you know. It blew him down the yard and split his jacket from top to bottom. The buggers couldn't kill him at Caparetto in 1918 but they've nigh done for him this time. It's a crying shame he's past it. Twenty years ago, he'd have seen them creatures off! Riff-raff. What's Hilter more than a housepainter, when all's said and done? Well, come in. If you can get in.

12

SCENE 17

(In **Grand-da's** *home. He is sitting in a chair in his pyjamas and an overcoat, and wearing a black beret with two badges. He points to one badge.)*

Grand-da. I knew I'd cop it last night. I dreamed HE came back for me.

Nana *(Explaining).* The Austrian soldier he killed with a bayonet in 1918. He can't forget him. Even the kettle lid rattling reminds him of the guns.

Grand-da *(Lost in a private nightmare, he is setting, aiming and firing a machine gun).* Range? Three Seven Five. Gun cocked. Two hundred rounds expended. Three boxes of ammo in reserve. Barrel cold, topped with water. Spare barrel in reserve. Half worn out, Sir.

(He braces himself rigid and then shakes as the 'ghost' gun fires)

Nana *(To* **The Others***).* He's taken it bad. He hasn't done this for years. He thinks they're coming for him.

Grand-da. Oh, my God! Breech jammed. . . Re-cock. Discharge. Re-cock!

*(***Grand-da***'s hands are now moving frantically)*

Nana. I'll mix him a powder. Give me a hand, Chas.

(They comfort and settle **Grand-da***)*

Dad. The taxi will be here any minute and the furniture van will be round soon. The furniture will be all right at the Repository, and you'll be all right with us.

Chas *(To* **Dad***).* Can I walk home?

Dad. Home by five. . . And stay away from that unexploded bomb!. . . Come on, Grand-da!. . . Help me out with him, Chas.

(They leave the bombed house. **Dad** *takes* **Grand-da***. As* **Nana** *goes, she takes a long lingering look round the room.)*

Chas *(Finding and putting on* **Grand-da***'s old helmet).* He loves this helmet. He wore it at Caparetto. Now! 'Range Three Seven Five. Gun cocked. Two hundred rounds expended. . . '

(In deadly earnest he aims his imaginary machine-gun at the sky. Then, with the helmet concealed, he follows **The Others.***)*

13

SCENE 18

*(In the school playground. **Boys** and **Girls** are playing — principally, in two gangs. **'Clogger' Duncan** and **'Nicky' Nichol** are there.)*

Cem *(To **Chas**).* You're mad.

Chas. No, I'm not. We got Clogger now.

Clogger. Oh, tripe.

Chas. Look, Sicky Nicky has something we need. We've got to make it worth his while.

Cem. Why do we have to build our camp in his garden?

Chas. Nobody goes there any more. Where else do you know that's private?

Clogger. So we walk home with Nicky, and Boddser will kick your head in.

Chas. We'll see. . .

> *(They approach **Nicky**. There is some banter. **Chas** says)*

. . . Evening, Knickers, my dear chap. How seems the world to you today? Want to come home with us?

> *(**Nicky** is very relieved and grateful)*

Boddser. Gerr-r-away, McGill! He's ours!

Chas *(To **Boddser**).* I beg your pardon, Oh Mighty One, Oh Star of the East, Oh Moon of My Delight. Your beauty dazzles me, Oh Four Eyes. . .

> *(**The Members of Boddser's Gang** enjoy this, a little)*

Boddser. Gerraway, McGill! I'm warning you! I've no quarrel with you. . . For now.

Chas. Oh, thank you! Thank you, Worshipful Lord! May Allah bless your luscious toe-nails!

Boddser *(To **His Gang**).* Get past them!

> *(**The Gang** blocks the exit)*

Cem. Told you so. Bloody fool, Chas!

Boddser. Right, McGill! You've asked for this!

> *(**Boddser** and **Chas** prepare to fight: rolling up their sleeves, and so on)*

Chas. Take your specs off. I don't want your Mum complaining to me Dad if I break them.

Boddser *(Mocking)*. Playing for time, McGill?

(He takes a swipe at **Chas,** *who ducks. Gravel is thrown, and* **Boddser** *crouches.* **Chas** *hits him with his gas-mask case, and, in a frenzy, beats him to the ground.)*

Cem *(To* **Chas***)*. You're bloody mad! Stop it! You'll kill him!

> *(*Clogger *pulls* **Chas** *away. Then he goes back to the whimpering* **Boddser.***)*

Clogger *(To* **Boddser***)*. Shut your noise! You'll live!. . . *(To* **The** Bystanders*)*. . . You'd better get him to hospital!

SCENE 19

(The schoolroom. **Liddell,** *with a cane, and* **Chas.***)*

Liddell. Britishers do not use weapons. They fight only with their fists. Bend over, Boy.

> *(He gives* **Chas** *six of the best)*

SCENE 20

(In **Nicky***'s garden.* **Nicky, Chas** *and* **Audrey** *are there. All look gloomy.)*

Nicky. Like to see my goldfish? It's six inches long.
Chas. Gerroff! They always die when they get too big for the jam jar.
Nicky. 'T isn't a jam jar. He's got a pond all to himself. He's four years old.
Chas. Yeah, and my pet rabbit's ninety-four. . .
Nicky *(Offering bread and butter)*. Here! Want some?
Audrey. Real butter! Where d'you get it?
Nicky. We've got ratings billeted on us. It comes off the destroyers. Everything comes off the destroyers.

> *(*Nicky *picks up an empty gin bottle)*

Chas *(Feeling sorry for him)*. What does your Mum do?
Nicky. Not much since my father got killed. His ship was torpedoed off Gibraltar. . . Have some more. . .
Chas and **Audrey.** Ta.

Nicky's Mother *(Calling, from a distance, in a haughty, wobbly voice. She has a glass in her hand).* What *are* you doing, Benjamin? What are you *doing?* Who are these *children?*

(She staggers slightly)

A Man's Voice. Fiona! What are you doing?

Nicky. That's the chap in charge of ratings. He lives here, too.

Nicky's Mother *(Calling again).* Mind you behave yourself, Benjamin. . .

(There is silence from the house)

Audrey *(Pointing).* Look! There's the fish! The goldfish!

*(**The Three** peer into the gloom)*

Nicky. There used to be twelve of them. My father imported them from China, but this is the only one left. He's called Oscar.

Audrey *(Softly).* Hello, Oscar.

Chas. He only talks Chinese. What's all them crosses in the rockery?

Nicky. My cats and dogs.

Chas. And what's that one?

Nicky. That's for my father. . .

*(**Audrey** kicks **Chas**)*

Chas. There's a good view from here. . . There's the bay, and the sea. . . I vote we make a secret camp here in the rockery. It'll be our fortress.

Audrey. Oh, yes! Please!

*(**Chas** and **Audrey** look to **Nicky**. He smiles and nods.)*

SCENE 21

*(In the school playground. **Chas, Cem, Carrots, Audrey** and **Other Boys** and **Girls** are arriving.)*

Cem *(Pointing to the school roof).* Blimey! Look at that! Right through the roof, too!

Chas. Dornier D.O. 17.

Cem. Garn! It's a Junkers 88.

Chas. 'T isn't. And I should know. It flew right down over Nicky's garden when me and Audrey were there yesterday. I had to throw myself on to her. . .

16

Cem. What!
Chas. Well, it was my duty, wasn't it?

(Liddell approaches.)

Liddell. Hello, McGill! After another machine gun?
Chas. Sir?
Liddell. Skip it.
Cem. What is it, Sir?
Liddell. I'll tell you what it is. It's an early start to the Christmas holiday for you. The petrol tank's burst and the school's full of fumes. One accidental spark, and up it goes!
Cem. Aren't we going to another school, Sir?
Liddell. No room. Two other schools copped it last night.

*(He goes away. The **Boys** and **Girls** hang about, aimlessly.)*

Audrey. A baby got born in our shelter last night.
Carrots. Congratulations! We didn't know you were expecting.

*(**Audrey** is embarrassed)*

Cem. Me Dad's busy. Some of the pensioners are dying in the shelters. Bronchitis. It's the damp.
Chas. Let's go and work on the fortress.

(There are groans, and then agreement)

*(During the next four scenes, **Chas** and **His Gang** silently build their fortress in **Nicky's Mother's** rockery)*

SCENE 22

*(Somewhere down town. **Air Raid Warden 'Fatty' Hardy** approaches* **The Police Sergeant.**)

Sergeant. Yes, Constable Hardy? What is it now?
Hardy. Strange bit of nicking on my patch. Hardly makes sense.
Sergeant. Well?
Hardy. Someone's pinching sandbags, Sarge. The ones we tied to the lamp-posts against incendiary bombs.
Sergeant. But they're the ones the dogs pee on. Nobody will touch those, even in an emergency.

17

Hardy. That's the point, Sarge. No one in their right mind would. Leaves only one conclusion. It's the work of enemy agents. . .

*(*__The Two Men__ *stare at each other as the scene fades)*

SCENE 23

(Outside **Nicky's Mother's** *house.* **Nicky's Mother** *is looking at her garden.)*

Nicky's Mother *(Calling).* Darling?
Nicky's Mother's Boyfriend-In-Charge-of-Ratings *(Off).* Yeah?
Nicky's Mother. Someone's stolen our air raid shelter. The one for the servants, down in the shrubbery.
Nicky's Mother's Boyfriend. So?
Nicky's Mother. Well, it's the principle of the thing. People seem to think they can do what they like with other people's property, these days. Everyone's gone so immoral — and all they do is blame it on the war. . .
Nicky's Mother's Boyfriend. Come back to bed. I'm on duty in half an hour.

(She turns to go to him as the scene fades)

SCENE 24

(A Home Guard Command Post. **Duty Officer 'Sandy' Sanderson** *is sitting by a phone.)*

D. O. Sanderson *(Picking up the phone).* HQ here. . . Yes, Petty Officer? Thieving, you say? Nothing new, Old Man. What's missing?. . . 'Three tin hats. Two fire buckets. One notice board. One stove. Paraffin heating. One stirrup pump'. . . Hardly the Black Market boys, Petty Officer. Not like nylons, or butter. Well. . . keep me briefed.

(He puts down the phone as the scene fades)

SCENE 25

(In the garden, outside **The McGills'** *shelter.* **Dad** *is working.* **Chas**
approaches.)

Chas. I'll help with that concreting, Dad.
Dad. Help me? You feeling all right?
Chas. I just feel like helping. I'd like to see how you do it.
Dad. Well, you won't see much. Some thieving swine has pinched half
    me cement. You wouldn't know anything about that?
Chas *(Innocently).* Me, Dad? No, Dad.

    (The Members of **Chas' Gang** *add another concrete block, with
    cement, to the fortress as the scene fades.)*

SCENE 26

(The fortress. **Chas's Gang** *are taking a tea break.* **Chas** *is wearing a
helmet.* **Clogger,** *in Scout uniform, also wears a helmet. All seem
    proud and satisfied as they survey their handiwork.)*

Chas. Standing Orders before we go?
The Members of the Gang. Standing Orders. . .
Chas. Fortress Caparetto! Standing Orders!

    *(*The Gang *stand. As* Chas *points to each member in turn they
    solemnly, but not without giggles, recite their rules):*

1 Anyone who steals from the fortress, if found guilty by court
   martial, shall be thrown in the goldfish pond. They may take
   off any clothes they want to, first, but keep it decent.
2 Anyone touching the gun without permission will be chucked
   out of the fortress for three months. Anyone who speaks to
   Boddser Brown for any reason will be chucked out for good.
3 Anyone lying on the bunks will tidy up afterwards.
4 No peeing within fifty yards, or anything else.
5 Always come in by the back fence, after making sure you're
   not followed.
6 No stealing from shops without permission. All goods stolen
   belong to the fortress.
7 Only sentries will touch the air rifle. Hand back all pellets out
   of your pockets, etc. when coming off duty.

19

8 Do not mess about with catapults inside the fortress or you
will wash up for four days.
9 Do not mess about at all.
10 Penalty for splitting to parents, teachers etc. is DEATH.
11 Do not waste anything.
12 Anyone who brings in useless old junk will take it back to the
tip where they got it.
13 Quartermaster gives out all the eats. Don't argue with her.

(Chas brings out the machine gun. Each puts a hand on it.)

All. We swear to keep these rules.
Nicky. I'm late. I must be home.
Chas. Yeah. Let's go. See you tomorrow.

(The fortress empties)

SCENE 27

*(In Nicky's house. It is dark. We hear — probably, from a tape — the
sounds of Nicky asleep. He is breathing deeply. He wakes with a start,
and is alarmed. He switches on his torch. There is silence. Then there
are the sounds of a man and a woman whispering and laughing.)*

Nicky *(Calling).* Mother!. . .

*(Sounds of the sea are accompanied by three foghorn blasts.
Nicky calls again)*

. . . Father!. . .

(He is in a state of panic. He shouts.)

. . . MOTHER! FATHER! . . .

(There is a loud explosion, followed by a complete blackout)

SCENE 28

*(The fortress in daylight, next morning. Chas stands in front of the
fortress, looking at the sky. Nicky, behind him, comes out of the
fortress.)*

Nicky. Chas?

Chas. Nicky! We all thought you were. . . How did you escape?

Nicky. My father came in a dream, and warned me. . . *(He takes a deep breath)*. . . They're all dead. Even the ratings. . . I went back and found them.

Chas. What'll you do now?

Nicky. I don't know. I suppose they'll put me in a home.

Chas. I wish you could stay with us. . . But Nana and Grand-da are staying with us till the end of the war.

Nicky. I don't want to leave this place. . . I mean. . . All this is mine, now. And I'd rather be with you than strangers.

(He holds out his hand to **Chas** *who takes it in both of his)*

Chas. We'll have a meeting. We'll see you through.

*(***Audrey, Cem, Clogger*** *and* **Carrots** *appear silently while* **Chas** *and* **Nicky** *are talking, and they listen)*

Nicky. I know where there's a lot of food. That Petty Officer who got killed was in the Black Market. Our old stables are full of the stuff.

Carrots. We'll have to tell a grown-up. They all think he's dead. It'll be on the records at the Town Hall. People will be worrying. . .

Clogger. Who? Who is there who cares?

Carrots. Grown-ups know what's best.

Clogger. Yeah, for grown-ups. They'll shove him in a home and forget him, like they did with me when my Mum died. They give you porridge without sugar and belt you if you leave your shoes lying around.

Audrey. He could stay with one of us. . .

Clogger. Would your mother have him?. . . *(***Audrey** *hangs her head. He asks* **The Others***)*. . . Would yours? Or yours?

(They hang their heads)

Cem. But where can he live?

Clogger. He could manage here. We've got grub for a year.

Carrots. Suppose he gets ill?

Clogger. Plenty of kids go to the doctor's on their own.

Carrots. But won't he get lonely?

*(***Nicky** *bursts into tears and babbles about 'Mother!' 'Father!' 'Hate!' 'Man!' and 'Death!'* **All the Boys** *look at* **Audrey***. She steps forward and shyly strokes* **Nicky's** *hair. Then, she repeats his name, gently.)*

21

Audrey *(To* **The Others***).* Everyone do it!

All. Nicky. . . Nicky. . . Nicky. . .

Nicky *(Eventually).* I'm all right, now. Sorry.

Clogger. I'll come and stay here, too. My Mum's cousin never wanted me, anyway. I'll be better off here.

Chas. Right! Everyone swear! On the gun! . . .

(They all place their hands on the gun, and **Chas** *says)*

. . . No one. . . Teachers, Mums, Dads, police, Germans. . . No one splits us up. . .

All. NO ONE!

(If AN INTERVAL is needed, this could be the right time)

SCENE 29

(Outside the **McGill** *house.* **The Police Sergeant** *approaches the house and knocks on the door.)*

Dad *(Answering).* What d'you want round 'ere again? Still after my kid's collection?

Sergeant. Look. We're worried about these kids. This war's doing bad things to kids. They're running wild. You don't know where you are with them, any more. These are decent kids from decent homes, but they go on more like slum kids with a Dad in the nick. You know. . . Against the police on principle.

Dad. Mebbe that says more about the police than the kids. . .

(He spits on the doorstep and turns to shut the door in **The Sergeant***'s face)*

Sergeant *(Jamming his foot in the door).* Look! They're up to something!

Dad. Take your foot out of my house! . . .

(The **Sergeant** *goes away. Then* **Dad***, worried, turns back into the house. After hesitating for a moment, he takes a Bible from a shelf and calls)*

. . . Chas! . . .

(Chas comes in, and **Dad** *says, wearily)*

. . . That policeman's been here again. I'm getting sick of them always knocking at our door. I want you to swear on the Bible

22

that you don't know anything about that machine-gun they keep on about. Here. . . *(He speaks in a tired voice)*. . . Put your hand on the Bible.

*(**Dad** slumps into a chair and yawns, looking away. He does not see that **Chas** has his hand raised above the Bible, not on it.)*

Chas *(Looking at the Bible as he speaks)*. I swear I don't know anything about a machine-gun.

*(**Dad**, still turned away, closes his eyes and sags visibly. **Chas** stands looking at **His Dad**, turns, and then goes quietly out towards the fortress.)*

SCENE 30

*(At the fortress. **Clogger**, looking through a telescope, is on watch. Near him are **Audrey**, **Cem**, **Carrots** and **Nicky**.)*

Clogger. Captain, Sir? . . . *(**Chas** looks out, and **Clogger** goes on)*. . .
Plane, Sir. Twin-engined, flying low.
Chas *(In alarm)*. Scarper! Gun out!

*(The gun is pushed out as **Clogger** scrambles back into the fortress)*

Clogger. Eh! Watch it! I don't want a hole where ma dinner is!

*(**Chas** grips the gun and peers down the gunsight)*

Chas. Oh, no! ANOTHER false alarm! Clogger, you been at your uncle's whisky again?
Clogger. There was something. Ah tell ye. It's too far off to see wi'out the telescope yet. Wait!

*(The sound of a plane increases in volume. **Chas** concentrates on the gunsight and **The Others** hold their breath as the plane passes overhead.)*
Cem. Go on! . . .

*(He nudges **Chas**, who releases the trigger. The gun fires. **Chas** falls backwards, taking the gun – still firing – with him. **The Others** cower down. Then the firing stops, the plane noise lessens, and anti-aircraft guns open up. **Cem** leaps up, saying)*

. . . Cor blimey! Pity we missed him!

23

Carrots. We didn't! We got him! We got him!

Audrey *(Scornfully).* You and how many Spitfires! You've certainly blown a fine hole in our roof with that thing!

(Chas stumbles to his feet. He is dazed, and holds his head. The gun has fallen apart.)

Chas. Stop squabbling, you two! A brave man has died. He died facing his foes. What more can any man hope for?

Audrey. What about that hole in the roof? And next time you might kill someone with that nasty great gun.

Chas. That's what it's for. That's what I was trying to do, so! Anyway, what do stupid girls know about it? Besides. . .

(He points at **Cem** *and says)*

. . . That stupid fool jogged my arm.

Cem. Weren't that. You couldn't hold the gun steady. You're puny, that's your trouble.

Chas. Nobody could have held it. It kicks like a mule. You haven't even tried firing it.

Audrey *(Again).* What about that hole in the roof? And, I'm not going back into the camp to make tea until you put that nasty great thing away.

Chas. Shut up, the lot of you! Anyway, it's broken. It kicked me back on to the ground and the spring has fallen out.

(The Gang gathers round the gun. Clogger lifts it.)

Clogger. You'd better find some way of mending this, if we're to stay as a company. It's our only defence. Let's do as she says, or we'll never get a cup of tea.

SCENE 31

(Somewhere in open country. **Rudi Gerlath,** *a rear-gunner, is making a landing by parachute. He hits the ground heavily.)*

Rudi *(In pain).* Aa-ch! My ankle! . . . *(He looks round, sees where he is, and says).* . . Rabbits! I envy you! Rabbits live longer than rear-gunners! . . . *(He looks at his ankle, sits, tries to move his ankle, and grimaces. Then he says to himself).* . . Can't walk. Might as well surrender. Might be a hot meal before interrogation. I'd reveal all the secrets of the Third Reich for a glass of Schnapps and a lump of sausage. . . *(He shouts loudly).* . . HEH!

(Nobody comes, so he curls up and sleeps)

SCENE 32

(A house damaged by bullets. **The Woman who lives there** *and* **Her Bed-ridden Mother** *are being visited by* **The Police Sergeant.***)*

The Woman *(Opening the door).* Ah, Sergeant! About time, too! I have a strange story to report to you. Come in quickly and sit down. . .

(She perches herself on the edge of a chair like a bird. Then she clasps her hands and closes her eyes.)

Sergeant *(Softly, under his breath).* Let us pray!

The Woman. Let us pray indeed, young man. For these are the Latter Days when the Foul Beast shall be loosed from the Pit. Book of Revelation, Chapter Thirteen, Verse Eleven. . . *(***The Sergeant** *raises his eyes Heaven-ward as* **The Woman** *goes on).* . . What is more, the servants of the Foul Beast have been machine-gunning my mother.

Sergeant. Your WHAT?

The Woman. Three days ago, as I live and breathe, I'd just taken Mother her cup of tea and was reading to her from the Good Book when something came through our roof and smashed the 'GOD IS LOVE' that hangs over her bed.

Sergeant *(Cautiously).* What sort of something? . . .

*(***The Woman** *digs in her purse and produces a flattened bullet.* **The Sergeant** *goes on).* . . What happened then?

The Woman. I ran to the window and saw their fearsome machine fleeing God's Wrath, going straight up into the Heavens.

Sergeant. German?

The Woman. It bore the Crooked Cross.

Sergeant *(Thoughtfully, and playing with the bullet).* What time did you say it occurred?

The Woman. I told you. Teatime. Are you the War Damage?

Sergeant. Am I WHAT?

25

The Woman. The War Damage. Mrs Spink said if I reported it to the War Damage, they'd come and mend the hole in our roof, and give us a new 'GOD IS LOVE'.

Sergeant. Madam, I am NOT the War Damage, but as I am here I will inspect the damage and report your claim to the appropriate quarters.

(He goes upstairs)

The Woman. Just you look up here. Nearly killed my mother, they did. . . Besides the damage to the 'GOD IS LOVE'. I'll leave you to inspect the damage.

(She goes away)

The Mother. 'Aven't gorra fag, 'ave ya? I'm right gasping. She won't let me 'ave them, yer know. Says they're 'ungodly'. Her and her God. She's potty, yer know. It's a case when a poor old body can't 'ave her death-bed comforts. . .

*(**The Sergeant** gives **The Mother** a cigarette and lights it. **The Mother**, smiling and sucking in smoke, says)*

. . . That's the first this week. Mrs Davies slips me one when she calls, but she's laid up with her sciatica.

Sergeant. Where d'you put the ash?

The Mother *(Pointing to the chamber pot)*. Last time the doctor came to test me water 'e nearly 'ad a fit.

Sergeant. Excuse me.

(He measures the distance between the holes in the ceiling. Then he looks along the tape and through the window.)

The Mother *(Gasping and coughing)*. Help!

*(She indicates the cigarette. **The Sergeant** takes it from her.)*

The Woman *(Returning, and seeing the cigarette in **The Sergeant**'s hand)*. This whole room stinks like the Foul Pit.

The Mother *(To her)*. I told 'im you wouldn't have smoking, Ada, but he wouldn't heed. He took advantage of me lying here 'elpless.

The Woman. So YOU say. I'll think my own thoughts about what happens to those who abuse God's Truth, on Judgement Day. Meanwhile, Officer, I'll ask you to leave. You're only here on sufferance. You're not even War Damage.

Sergeant. Madam, I have my job to do, and I am doing you a favour.

26

The Woman. Look at all me plaster. On me best carpet. Get out, or I'll set the police on you!

Sergeant *(Backing away).* Madam, I AM the police.

The Woman *(Shrieking).* Have you got a search warrant?

*(**The Sergeant** goes, muttering)*

SCENE 33

*(Near some back gardens. **Rudi** examines his ankle. He finds that he can stand and walk. He takes his pistol from its holster, examines it, and takes a trial aim. Then he fastens a sack round his middle.)*

Rudi *(To himself).* I must try to find a boat and escape, or else I'll give myself up. I can't spend the rest of the war with these rabbits. . . *(He speaks to the rabbits).* . . Goodbye, my friends!

*(He sets off, humming to himself in a monotonous way. Stout **Mrs Flynn** approaches. She is on her way to her dustbin with a plateful of scraps.)*

Mrs Flynn *(Seeing **Rudi** looking with longing at the scraps).*

Where YOU from?

*(**Rudi** talks gibberish, points to the plate and then to his mouth. **Mrs Flynn** offers the plate to him. He claws the scraps into his mouth.)*

Mrs Flynn. Wait a minute!

*(She goes away, and then returns with some bread and an apple. Thin, prim **Miss Smith** is following her.)*

Miss Smith. What's he want, Mrs Flynn? . . . *(To **Rudi**, she says).* . . What you hanging round here for, pestering women?

Rudi *(In an earnest voice).* Meerp! Meerp! Ugamea!

Mrs Flynn. Sshh, Miss Smith! Can't you see he's a dumbie?

Miss Smith *(With scorn).* Riff-raff! I'd shoot the likes of those! They're no use to the War Effort at all.

Mrs Flynn *(To her).* How much use are you, always on the Sick with your nerves? Leave the poor thing alone. He's not doing you any harm. . . *(She gives the bread and the apple to **Rudi** and says).* . . Here y'are, Love, and the best of luck.

27

Rudi. Ug! Ug! Meerp!

(*He shambles off.* **The Two Women,** *bickering, go away. Then* **Rudi** *approaches the area of* **Nicky**'*s garden and the fortress. There, he prepares to sit and eat the bread and apple.*)

SCENE 34

(*The fortress.* **Chas and His Gang** *see* **Rudi. Chas** *grabs the machine-gun.* **Rudi** *puts his hands in the air.*)

Chas. Quick! It's a Jerry! Get his gun!

(**Clogger** *gets behind* **Rudi** *and frisks him.* **Clogger** *takes* **The German**'*s pistol, and backs away.*)

Rudi. Please, hands down? Mein arms tired are.
Clogger *(Shouting).* Hande hock!

(*He cocks the pistol.*)

Rudi *(Carefully and slowly).* Please, may I down sit? I tired am.
Chas. Let him, Clogger. It's safer.

(**Clogger** *nods at* **Rudi,** *indicating the ground.* **Rudi** *sits down and puts his hands on the back of his neck.*)

Cem *(Wildly).* What are we going to DO? He's a Nazi!
Clogger. He don't look like a proper Nazi.
Carrots. He ain't got no swastikas.
Clogger. He's not a blond beast!
Audrey. He looks hungry. Can I give him a mug of tea?
Chas. Suppose so.

(**Rudi** *sucks noisily at the tea. He is very tired.*)

Cem. What are we going to do with him?
Carrots. Take him to the Wardens' Post.
Chas. What? With a loaded Luger stuck in his back? That'll cause a few
 questions. Besides, he'd tell them about us.
Nicky. But he can't talk English.
Clogger. He can, a bit. Besides, they'll interrogate him in German.
 Then he'll split about the fortress and the machine-gun, and then
 we've had it.

28

Chas. But they're only supposed to give their name, rank and number. That's in the Geneva Convention.

Cem. The what?

Chas. The Geneva Convention.

Cem. What do you know about the Geneva Convention?

Chas. My Dad told me.

Clogger. Och, tripe.

Cem. That only means he mustn't tell the interrogators anything about Germany. It doesn't mean he won't split on us.

(**Rudi,** *who has been watching their faces, starts to nod wearily.*)

Audrey *(Seeing this).* Hey! He's falling asleep!

Chas. Better get him inside. . . *(He calls to* **Rudi***).* . . Hey! Raus! RAUS!

(**Rudi** *jerks into wakefulness*)

Clogger. Poor devil! He's knackered!

(**Clogger** *points to a bunk in the fortress.* **Rudi** *staggers to it, and collapses into sleep.* **The Gang** *stand round in silence, gazing at* **Rudi***.*)

SCENE 35

(The **McGill** *kitchen.* **Dad, Mum, Nana** *and* **Chas** *are having breakfast.)*

Dad *(Reading a newspaper).* It's getting near the Spring Tides. That's when they'll come. Mark my words!

Mum. But it's not Spring, yet. It's only February.

Dad. I don't mean that kind of Spring, Woman. A Spring Tide's when the sea's higher than usual. It'll carry their flat-bottomed barges up over the beach defences.

Chas. What's flat-bottomed barges, Dad?

Dad *(Putting down his newpaper).* They're boats wi' flat bottoms, so that they can get close ashore. Hitler's gathering all he can find in Holland and Belgium. When he's ready, he'll tow them across, full of soldiers, using tugs.

Mum. But they won't come this far north. They'll land on the Thames, or Liverpool, or somewhere.

(**Chas** *laughs at* **His Mother***'s poor geography)*

29

Dad. Hah! Maybe that's what Hitler and them wants us to think. They'll get all our soldiers down south and then they'll attack up here and cut the country in half.

Mum. Don't talk like that, or I shan't sleep safe in my bed.

Nana. That Hilter's liable to do anything. Crafty. I reckon they don't watch the beach close enough. Hilter could nip ashore off one of them U-boats and we'd never know he was here till he walked in the front door. And then I'd tell him a thing or two. I haven't forgotten Grand-da's best top-coat and them two china dogs they done for.

Dad *(Patiently)*. Mother! Hitler wouldn't come on his own. He'd bring his whole army.

Nana *(Thinking)*. Mmmmm. . . Ah only wish Grand-da was twenty years younger. He'd see him off.

Chas. Do you really think they'll come, Dad?

Dad. Well, Hitler can't afford to hang about for ever. We're getting stronger all the time. There's all those Canadian soldiers arriving on the newsreels. And, we're churning out more and more Spitfires.

Nana *(Unimpressed)*. Spitfires is too fond of flying about all day like paper kites. It needs someone like your Grand-da to see that Hilter off. I'm telling ya.

SCENE 36

*(In the fortress. It is morning, but **Rudi** is still asleep. **Audrey** and **Nicky** are watching him. **Clogger** brings him a plate of food.)*

Clogger *(Waking **Rudi**)*. Here's ya breakfast.

*(**Rudi** sits up. He is shivering and coughing.)*

Audrey. He's poorly.

Clogger. He's got the bronchitis, Ah'm thinking.

Audrey. Do you think he'll die? Should we fetch a doctor?

Nicky. NO. They'll make me go into a home.

Audrey. I know! We've got some cough mixture at home. I'll go and fetch it.

(She leaves the fortress)

(The Home Guard Command Post. **Duty Officer Sanderson** *greets*
Liddell *as the teacher walks in.)*

D.O. Sanderson. 'Morning, Sar. Lovely morning. Think it's the day for
    Jerry? Two letters came for you, Sar. Poster from Northern
    Command about disguised German paratroops. And an offer of
    two shotguns from Farmer Moulton at Preston.
Liddell. Sounds good.
D.O. Sanderson. They are, Sar. They are. Came up nicely with a drop of
    oil. No ammo., though. But I think I can win some from a mate at
    the War Ag. Told him we were terrible pestered with rabbits.
Liddell *(Shocked).* Sarnt Major!
D.O. Sanderson. It's all for the War Effort, Sah. Jerry could be here by
    lunch. Can't go over the top without ammo., Sah. Oh, and there's a
    civvy policeman to see you, Sar.

    (**'Fatty' Hardy** *comes in)*

Liddell *(To* **Hardy***).* Oh, not you again? . . . *(He sounds irritated as he*
    says). . . It's not that machine-gun trouble again?
Hardy. 'Fraid so. Audrey Parton's parents have been complaining. Stays
    out till all hours. Comes home filthy. I've tried questioning her.
    Won't open her mouth to anyone.
Liddell. That'll be Audrey Parton of 3A at our school?
Hardy. Yes. And McGill's in 3A. And Jones his little mate. And the
    Nichol boy, who was supposed to be killed by that bomb. And
    Clogger Duncan, who ran off to Glasgow.
Liddell. 'Supposed'? But surely the Nichol boy IS dead?
Hardy. If he is, he's the first case I've heard of, of death by bombing,
    that never left a trace. And young Duncan never showed up in any
    of his old Glasgow haunts. We checked.
Liddell. So. . . ?
Hardy. They've got that gun and they've built a hideout for it.
    Remember those sandbags that went missing? And Nichol and
    Duncan are living there, and the others are keeping them fed. I've
    checked the families. The McGills keep on finding the odd pint of
    paraffin missing. The Partons are some candles short, and the
    Joneses a hurricane lamp.
Liddell. Told your Inspector about all this?

Hardy. I've tried. Trouble is, Mr McGill keeps on complaining that we're harrassing his son.

Liddell. And are you?

Hardy. We've tried to follow him. No hope. He led us a dance for ten miles. He finished up throwing pebbles at tin cans in the river. You might as well try shadowing a seagull. But we've got to find that gun. Another two feet and they'd have killed that old woman. Can't you think of something, Sir?

Liddell. But they know me better than they know you. . . Oh, let me think about it. . .

(As **Hardy** *goes out,* **Liddell** *moves towards* **Duty Officer Sanderson,** *who is looking out through binoculars.* **Liddell** *says to him)*

. . . All quiet, Sandy?

D.O.Sanderson. Yes, Sar. All quiet.

Liddell. Pass me the binoculars. . . *(He takes them, and then says).* . . Mmmm. . . These are strong. You can see the Square. That's where McGill lives. . . Mmmm. . . Interesting.

SCENE 38

(The fortress. **Clogger,** *with the pistol on his lap, is reading a comic while he is on guard over* **Rudi.***)*

Rudi *(Worried by the pistol).* Achtung! Pistole!

Clogger *(Waving the pistol at* **Rudi***).* Watch it!

Rudi *(Putting up his hands and then nervously miming the firing of a pistol).* . . BANG!. . . *(He imitates the sound of a bullet ricocheting round the fortress, finally entering his body, and then* **Clogger's***).* . . Tot! All dead! See!

*(***Clogger** *nods, and looks thoughtfully at the pistol.* **Rudi** *mimes the suggestion that he should be tied up securely by the wrists.)*

Clogger *(Calling).* Nicky! Bring your bike padlock!. . .

*(***Nicky** *brings a padlock and chain, and* **Clogger** *says).* . . I don't trust him and I can't make out what he's trying to tell us.

Nicky. I'll do it.

(Timidly, he chains **Rudi** *to a bunk)*

32

Clogger *(Holding the pistol away from himself, and trying to uncock it).* Like this?

Rudi. Nein! Nein!. . . *(He mimes the correct procedure).* . . So!

Clogger. Here! Look! That right?. . . *(They all smile as the earlier tension is relaxed. Then* **Clogger** *says, with a strange pronunciation).* . . 'Pistole'?

Rudi *(Repeating this correctly).* Pistole.

Clogger *(Trying it).* Pistole?

Rudi. Ja! Gut!. . . *(They laugh. Then* **Rudi** *points to a mug and says).* . . Krug!. . . *(He points to a hurricane lamp and says).* . . Sturmlampe!. . . *(They are laughing, again, as* **Chas** *and* **The Other Members** *of* **His Gang** *come in)*

Clogger *(Showing them the pistol).* Did you know this 'pistole' has got a safety catch? And this 'krug'. . . *(He points to the mug, and says)* . . . Is for tea? How about it, Audrey?

Audrey. Always the same! Can't you men learn to make tea? You'll never win the war without it. . . *(She nods at* **Rudi,** *and asks).* . . What's he chained up for?

Nicky. We weren't sure if he was trying to escape, but he was trying to tell us how to make the gun safe. . . *(***Nicky** *hesitates, and then goes on).* . . I like him. Can I unchain him and give some tea?

(All nod, so **Nicky** *unchains* **Rudi** *and then goes to help* **Audrey** *with the tea)*

Chas *(To* **Rudi***).* You. . . feel. . . better? *(***Chas** *pretends to cough).* . . Better? No cough?

*(***Rudi** *nods. Then, as all drink tea,* **Carrots** *picks up* **Clogger***'s comic and shares it with* **Rudi.** *After giving* **Rudi** *a mug of tea,* **Nicky** *leans on him and he, too, looks at the comic.)*

Rudi. Was ist 'Dospreet Dan?

Carrots *(Explaining).* Dan. . . *(He points at a picture).* . . Rudi. . . *(He points at* **Rudi***).* . . Nicky. . . *(He points at* **Nicky***)*

Rudi. But 'Dospreet? Was ist das?. . . *(***Carrots** *rolls his eyes wildly, and pretends to tear his hair, so* **Rudi** *asks).* . . A nutter?

Carrots. Nein. No.

Rudi. But why 'Dospreet' is he? In these stories he is always winning.

*(***Everyone** *laughs)*

Nicky. Give us a song, Rudi.

(All want **Rudi** *to sing. So, he gives them 'Ich hatt' einen kameraden!' and* **The Members of the Gang** *take up the words of the sad old soldiers' song.)*

Clogger *(Interrupting).* Hey, belt up, you lot! Someone might hear us!

(As **Rudi** *goes back to the comic,* **Chas** *and* **Clogger** *look at the machine-gun. Then, with glances at* **Rudi,** *they start to argue.)*

Chas. I tell you we CAN make him work. It's in the Geneva Convention.
Clogger. Yah, bunkum! You can't make a prisoner-of-war help you against his own people.
Chas. You can if it's not war work. I know a farmer's got two Italians. They mend walls and milk cows and things. . . *(He speaks to* **Rudi).** . . Rudi! You know about guns and things. . . *(He shows him the machine-gun).* . . This gun is jammed, and we need it. You could mend our machine-gun if you wanted to.
Rudi. Ha! What will you do to me if I do not mend it?
Cem. We could shoot you.
Rudi. I, the Geneva Convention plead. Prisoners-of-war are never shot.

(**The Gang** *shout 'That's right!' and turn on* **Cem.***)*

Cem. Well. . . We could hand you over to the Army!
Rudi *(Laughing).* So many questions, they would ask. Interrogate me with rubber hoses and bright lights, like in the American movies. I spill the beans might.

(Everyone laughs)

Clogger. We do want the gun mended, though. It's important.
Chas. We wouldn't fire it, promise. Except at Ger. . . *(Chas stops suddenly. He had forgotten that* **Rudi** *was a German).* . . Anyway, we wouldn't fire it. It's our mascot.
Rudi *(Thinking hard of his own needs).* I do you a deal. I need a boat. You, a sailing boat get, and I the gun will mend.

SCENE 39

(The Home Guard Command Post. **Liddell,** *looking through binoculars, gives a commentary to* **Duty Officer Sanderson.***)*

Liddell. Interesting, Sandy. It's McGill again. Every morning he's off on this cat and mouse game, but I can never see where he gets to.

34

Hello! Someone's following him! I told that fool police sergeant to lay off. He's bright, that lad. He knows he's being followed. Look, Sandy! See how he's doubled back? You look. Can you see who it is?

D.O.Sanderson *(Taking the binoculars).* No, Sar! But it's not Hardy or the sergeant.

SCENE 40

(On some mud flats, near the town. **Chas,** *trying to escape from his pursuer, turns and sees that it is* **Boddser,** *who then attacks and flattens* **Chas.***)*

Chas. Gerroff, you swine!
Boddser. Poor old Chassy McGill! Where's your brains now, Chas?. . . *(He twists* **Chas***'s arm, and says).* . . Why don't you shout for help? Go on! Shout!
Chas. Ger-r-off! *(He shouts).* . . Help!
Boddser. Right! Now, where's that machine-gun?. . .

(Gasping and squirming, **Chas** *throws* **Boddser** *off him. Then he crawls to the edge of the acting area and lies with his head hanging over.* **Boddser** *flattens him again.)*

. . . Thank you, McGill. That's saved me a lot of trouble. . .

(He pushes **Chas***'s head down, as though under water.* **Chas** *gasps and swears as he catches breath. Then he bites* **Boddser***'s hand.* **Boddser** *lets go, but* **Chas** *lies, apparently exhausted. Then* **Boddser** *asks)*

. . . Want some more, McGill?

*(***Chas***'s silence frightens* **Boddser.** *He shakes* **Chas,** *who leaps up, and, running by a circuitous route, approaches the fortress.* **Boddser** *is close behind him.)*

35

(At the fortress)

Chas *(Shouting).* Clogger!. . . CLOGGER!

   *(***Boddser** catches **Chas***)*

Boddser. So, we start again, McGill! Where's that machine-gun?

Chas. No, we won't! Look behind you!

Boddser. Think I'd fall for that trick, Stupid?

Clogger *(Appearing behind* **Boddser***).* Perhaps you'd better!

Boddser *(Turning).* Clogger Duncan! But you went home to Glasgow!

Clogger. Some people thought I did. . . *(To* **Chas***).* . . What shall we do with him, Chas?

Chas. He's been torturing me! Getting me to tell about the gun.

Boddser. Now, wait. . . *(He backs away into the arms of* **Carrots** *and* **Cem,** *and says).* . . It's none of your business. It was a fair fight. One against one.

Carrots. When did you fight fair?. . . *(To* **Chas***).* . . It's up to you, Chas. We can't afford this lad any more. Shall we do him proper?

Chas. Do him proper.

   *(***Chas** *watches as* **Boddser** *is pushed from fist to fist until he falls down and is sick)*

Clogger. Had enough?. . . *(***Boddser** *nods, so* **Clogger** *says).* . . Aye! Enough for now! Enough till ye get home and blab to your mother that I'm still in Garmouth, and where I'm living, and that Chas knows all about it. You know where the machine-gun is now, don't you? And your precious mother'll run straight to the police.

Boddser *(Mumbling).* They'll send you away to Borstal. All of you.

Carrots. If you tell them.

Boddser. Try and stop me!

   (The **Gang** *kick him until he screams in agony and is sick again)*

Clogger *(To* **Boddser***).* You can put us all in Borstal, but you can't keep us there! And I'll get out, and when I do I'll come looking for you, Boddser Brown. And I'll finish off what we've started today. Ye understand me, Brown? I'll kill you, if I swing for it!

   (The **Gang** *leave* **Boddser** *lying in front of the fortress as they go inside.)*

SCENE 42

(Outside the **McGills'** *home.* **Liddell** *walks up and knocks.)*

Mum *(Answering)*. Why, hello, Mr Liddell! Do you want Charles? You'll have to go up to the bedroom, I'm afraid. He came home in a right muck last night. Thick wi' mud and soaked to the skin. He can't raise his arms above his head this morning, and he looks like someone's been at his eyes wi' a blacking brush. Expect he's been fighting again. You know what lads are.

Liddell. I am sorry to hear that, Mrs McGill. I won't disturb him now. Try to keep him quiet for a few days.

(He goes away)

SCENE 43

(Outside the **Browns'** *home.* **Liddell** *walks up and knocks.)*

Mrs Brown *(Answering)*. Mr Liddell! I was just thinking of calling the police, but you'll do as well. Bernard came home in a shocking state last night. He was soaked to the skin and plastered with mud from head to foot. He's been crying all morning. I've had the doctor to him. You should see his poor little ribs — they're black and blue. He won't say a word, but a mother knows. It's those big lads been at him again. That Charles McGill. I don't know what the world's coming to, with all this hooliganism. You should just see his bruises, poor mite.

Liddell. I wouldn't advise the police, Madam. I've just come from the McGill house, and he's in just the same state. What's more, your son's as big as McGill, and I happen to know he started the business. We've enough trouble fighting the Germans, without the children trying to kill each other. Good afternoon, Madam!

(He goes away)

SCENE 44

(In the fortress. **Rudi** *is asleep.* **The Gang** *are trying to persuade* **Nicky** *to part with* **His Father***'s boat.)*

Nicky. I never went sailing with my father before the War.

Cem. Yes, you did. You used to boast about it at school. And I saw you out with him once. It was a boat with a red sail.

Nicky. He hired that from a fisherman.

Chas. No, he didn't. You told me he had his own boathouse on the river.

Nicky *(Stubbornly)*. It got bombed.

Carrots. Where was it, then?

(Everyone stares at **Nicky**, *who fidgets uncomfortably)*

Nicky. All right. It's still there. At Prior's Haven. But the key to the boathouse got lost when our house was bombed.

Clogger. It'll no matter. We'll force the lock.

Nicky *(Muttering, in an ashamed way)*. It's all right. I've got the key here.

(He puts his hand inside his shirt and pulls out a key on a string)

Clogger. For Hell's sake! What's the matter with ye? Are ye part of this gang or no?

Nicky *(Snivelling)*. It's my boat. It's my father's boat.

Clogger. Well, if that's the case, I'll be away home to Glasgow tomorrow. I can't afford to hang round here all ma life. Ye can have the fortress, Nicky, all of it. That's yours as well. And you can sort out Rudi as you think fit. Ah'll pack my things.

(He moves away. **Nicky** *looks round for support, but* **The Other Members of the Gang** *avoid his gaze.)*

Chas. Sorry, Nicky, but we've got to give Rudi that boat, 'cos otherwise he won't mend that gun. And the Germans are coming soon, and we'll need it.

Nicky. Who says the Germans are coming?

Chas. My Dad. He says if they don't come soon, they won't be able to come, and then they'll have to admit they've lost the War.

Carrots. Everyone knows they're coming.

Cem. The soldiers dug pits on our soccer field to make their gliders crash.

Audrey. The BBC said vicars had to ring the church bells when they come.

Nicky *(Hopelessly)*. Oh, all right. What do you want me to do?

Chas *(Slightly embarrassed)*. Take us and show us where the boat is.

Nicky. But I can't go out. People will recognise me.

38

Clogger. Here! Take this balaclava helmet! You'll pass for a slum kid like me. You're mucky enough.

(They move towards the boathouse)

SCENE 45

(In **The McGills'** *shelter.* **Mum, Chas, Mrs Spalding** *and* **Colin** *are there. It is during a black-out, and an air raid is in progress.)*

Mrs Spalding. They've got the Docks, this time.

*(***Mum** *knits furiously, with a set face)*

A Voice. Ashington's been hit. There's fifty men trapped by a bomb down the Rising Sun Colliery.

Mrs Spalding. Ashington's been hit. They're all trapped. . . *(She listens, and then says). . .* South Shields gas holder's been hit. You can see it burning!. . . *(She listens again). . .* What's that?

Mum *(In an icy voice).* What do you THINK you hear, Mrs Spalding?

Mrs Spalding *(Hesitating).* I. . . I thought I heard the church bells ringing.

(All listen. Bells can be heard, in the distance.)

Mum. It must be some mistake.

Chas. Mum! I want to go to the lav.!

Mum. Not now. You can hear the bells. You know what it means.

Chas. But, Mum, I'll wet myself! The Germans aren't here, yet. . . There's time. . . Mum! I'm bursting!

Mum *(Screaming at him).* All right! Go!

SCENE 46

(In the fortress. **Rudi** *is there. Church bells are ringing, and the air raid goes on.* **Clogger** *runs in.)*

Clogger. Rudi! They're here! It's time to go!

(Then **Chas** *arrives, breathless, followed by* **Cem, Audrey, Carrots** *and* **Nicky,** *one at a time and all talking at once)*

Chas. Do you hear the bells? We've got to get the gun operational.

39

Clogger. Yes, Captain! Glad you've got here!

Cem. My Dad's taken cover in the Cemetery. I couldn't stand the smell.

Audrey. We were running away. The Partons were running away!

Carrots. Mine ran to the Church. I feel safer here.

Clogger. Shut up! You heard what Chas said! We need the gun!

> *(He hands the gun to* **Rudi** *who takes it reluctantly, puts it together, and cocks it)*

Chas. So that's how you cock it. That's what we did wrong. We forgot to re-cock it! Now, who'll take Rudi to the boat?

Nicky. I will.

> *(They all shake hands. Then* **Nicky** *and* **Rudi** *leave the fortress.)*

Audrey. Let's sing, quietly.

> *(They sing 'Ich hatt' einen kameraden', and a lot of tears are surreptitiously flicked from faces)*

SCENE 47

(The **McGill** *kitchen.* **Grand-da** *and* **Nana** *are there, in the dark, when* **Mum** *comes in with a torch.)*

Mum *(Calling).* Chas! Chassy!

A Voice from the Dark. Here!

Mum *(Spotlighting* **Grand-da** *and* **Nana***).* Chassy?

Nana. No. It's me and Grand-da, Love.

Mum. What are you doing? Why aren't you down the shelter?

Nana. Grand-da and me's waiting for the Jarmans, Love. I've got the bread knife and he's got the carving knife.

Mum. But they'll shoot you, first!

Nana. Aye, well, they can shoot us both together. Forty years, we've had, and they're not separating us into those consecration camps at our age. We'll go together, sink or swim. . . *(***Grand-da** *coughs, and* **Nana** *says to him).* . . Hey, Man! Wrap yourself up better! You'll catch your death!

Mum. You should be in bed, Grand-da.

Grand-da. Nay, Lass. I'll face them brutes on me feet, like I always did.

Mum. Chassy's run off somewhere. I can't find him. He said he was going to the lav., but he's gone.

Nana. He'll be off to the fighting, maybe. McGills always went to the fighting young. Grand-da here volunteered to fight the Boers when he was only sixteen.

Mum *(Screeching).* Oh, Nana, he CAN'T have!

Nana. Rest yourself, Love. If the Jarmans don't come, he'll be home by morning. And if they do, he'll have as much chance as everybody else.

*(**Mum** runs out, crying 'Chas!')*

SCENE 48

*(The Home Guard Command Post. **Dad** and **Liddell** are there, with **Duty Officer Sanderson** and **The Police Sergeant**.)*

Dad *(Speaking into the telephone).* Two houses demolished in Emily Street. Gas main fractured. Possibly three people trapped in wreckage. At least one still alive. . . *(He looks up, sees that **His Wife** has come into the Post, and says).* . . Maggie!

Mum. Chas has run off somewhere. I can't find him. Please come and help me look.

*(She starts to cry. **D.O. Sanderson** passes a report to **Dad**, who picks up the phone.)*

Dad *(Trying to read the report).* 'Boy lying injured in front garden of 11 Wimbledon Terrace. . . No. That's 17 Wimbledon Terrace. . . Boy can't move. Suspected fractured spine. Ambulance essential'. . .

*(**Mum**, sobbing, collapses. **Dad** says to her)*

. . . Stop it, Love. It mightn't be him. He might be all right.

Mum *(Screaming at him).* Come and look! Come and help me! Help me! Help me! I don't know what to do!

*(**D.O. Sanderson** passes another report to **Dad**, who takes it and picks up the phone again)*

Dad *(Reading).* 'Outbreak of fire in warehouse in Dock Road. Building contains bales of cloth. No noxious fumes as yet. Fire in danger of spreading to nearby paraffin store. Dock Road blocked by

41

rubble'. . . (*He tries to look at a map.* **Mum** *is standing in front of it. He shouts*). . . For God's sake get this woman out of here!

(**D.O. Sanderson** *and* **The Sergeant** *take* **Mum***'s arms, but gently*)

D.O. Sanderson. Hey! Steady up, Ma'am!

Mum (*Bitterly, to* **Dad***).* Your own son, and you wouldn't look for him! God forgive you, for I never shall!

(*Sobbing, she runs off*)

Dad (*Almost in a whisper*). 'Fire engine gone to Dock Road.'

(*He sticks a pin in the map. For a moment, all are busy. Then the phone rings, breaking the silence.* **Liddell** *picks it up.*)

Liddell. Command Post. Mullins? What? Jerry's landed? We'll pick up the Reserves and be over. By the bridge at Blyth? Right!. . . (*He puts the phone down, and says*). . . Come on, Sandy! Sergeant!

(*They rush out*)

SCENE 49

(*Near the sea.* **Nicky** *and* **Rudi** *enter.* **Rudi** *is holding oars.*)

Nicky. The boat's moored over there. Use your oars till you get clear of the Castle Cliff. Then pull on the rope to raise the big sail.

Rudi. Right. Thanks a lot, Nicky. . . For the boat.

Nicky. It was my Dad's boat. I wish you were my Dad. Can't I come with you?

Rudi. Nein. Where I go, no place for you is.

Nicky (*Urging*). I could sail the boat for you. I'm an expert, honest. Only. . . the boat's going and you're going. . . and there's nothing left.

Rudi. Nein, Liebling. There is much left — your kamerads, your gun, your country.

Nicky. But I like you better. Better even than my father.

Rudi. And I you. But we both our duties have. Perhaps I see you after the War. Then we all kamerads be?

(**Nicky** *starts to cry as* **Rudi** *leaves. Then* **Nicky** *hears the noise of the oars in the water, and cries uncontrollably.*)

42

SCENE 50

(In the open, near a 'pillbox'. **Liddell** *leads forward* **Duty Officer Sanderson, The Police Sergeant** *and* **The Reserves.** *They are met by* **Sergeant Mullins.***)*

Mullins. They're on the road, Sir, beyond the bridge. In lorries, they are. They've stopped at the moment. Mr Whiteload's talking to the fellow who seems to be in charge.

Liddell. Talking?

Mullins. They're trying to bluff their way through, I reckon. They can't know how little we've got inside this pillbox, can they?

Liddell. How do you know they're Germans?

Mullins. They're foreigners, for sure — you should hear 'em babble. And they haven't got no movement order. Mr Whiteload asked them for that, straight away.

*(***Liddell** *signs to* **D.O. Sanderson,** *who hurries away. Then* **Mr Whiteload** *approaches. With him is* **Major Koslowski,** *of the Polish Free Army.* **Koslowski** *is gesturing dramatically.)*

Whiteload *(To* **Liddell***).* I'm glad you're here, Sir. This officer says he is Major Er. . . Er. . .

Koslowski. Koslowski. Stanislaus Koslowski, Major, Polish Free Army, at your service. . . *(He clicks his boots together, and says).* . . I am ruddy marvellously amazed to make your acquaintance, Colonel.

Liddell. What are you chaps doing on the move without a movement order?

Koslowski. Ve no vait for any ruddy movement order. Germans come — is enough. We go kill ruddy Germans. Do ve need a killing-Germans-order also? Poles can kill Nazis without orders.

Liddell. Look, Old Lad. If everyone goes off half-cock without orders, we shall have chaos.

Koslowski. Ho, yes, Englishman. You want everything nice and neat. Like your ruddy privet hedges. Like your wife's kitchen at home. My wife not at home. Wife and children is dead, road out of Warsaw. Nazi fighter shoots them into very small bits. Not neat, eh?

*(***Duty Officer Sanderson** *returns breathlessly, and salutes)*

D.O. Sanderson. Hold everything, Sar! This lot IS the Polish Army.

HQ knows all about them. But there isn't any German invasion.
Some short circuit in a police telephone box at Blyth started the
bell ringing. It's all snowballed from there.
Liddell *(To* Koslowski*).* Tell your chaps to pack up and go home.
You're wasting petrol.
Koslowski. If Germans come, we find more petrol. In Blyth we for
Germans will look.

*(*Koslowski *marches off, shouting orders in some 'foreign'
language)*

SCENE 51

(The Home Guard Command Post. Dad *is still there when* Liddell
returns.)

Dad. What a night! And now it's all over. . . Until it starts up again.
Liddell *(Tired and exhausted).* These Poles will be the death of me.
They're convinced Jerry landed last night, and to prove their
point they're on the rampage through Blyth. Any news of your
lad?
Dad. No. . . And Constable Hardy has just called in to say several
other kids are missing, and he's organising a search party. I'm
off to look for Chas.

(He turns to go, meeting, as he does so, Koslowski*)*

Koslowski. Officer! The best of good mornings! How am I able to
help you?
Dad. Perhaps your men could help us to search for some children who
are missing. . .

('Fatty' Hardy *enters, and* Liddell *says to him)*

. . . Constable! This Polish officer and his men will help in the
search party.

*(*Dad *goes out)*

Koslowski. Ah, yes! Helping we most certainly will! We form a line
down to the beach, huh? And sweeps toward that bombed house,
huh? Yes, my men could doings with a walk. They are cooped up
all night. We find no Jerries nowhere.

44

(He shouts some orders to **His Men**. *Then, with* **Koslowski** *leading them, and followed by* **Hardy**, **The Men** *fan out and search through* **The Audience** *for* **The Children**. *In 'foreign' voices, they call to each other.)*

SCENE 52

(In the fortress. **Chas** *and* **The Gang** *are asleep. Then* **Chas** *wakes. He remembers the night before and peers out anxiously over some sandbags. Then he sees the advancing* **Poles**.*)*

Chas *(Raising the alarm)*. Clogger! Carrots! Wake up! They've come! Jerry's here!. . .

 *(***The Gang*** *wake; leap up; and seize any available weapons. Then* **Chas** *calls out)*

 . . . Load! Cock! Range?
Clogger. They're up to the white fence.
Chas. That's three-fifty yards.
Clogger. Three hundred.
Chas. Go on! I've paced it hundreds of times.
Clogger. Yer puny pace is never a yard!
Chas. 'Tis!

 (He settles behind the machine-gun)

Cem *(Looking out)*. Hey! 'Fatty' Hardy's with them! Pointing things out to them.
Clogger. He's a Quisling.*
Cem. Perhaps he's their prisoner.
Clogger. We can't help that. Fire before they're right on top of us!

 *(***Chas*** *fires.* **The Poles**, *startled, drop down and adopt 'battle positions')*

Hardy. Eh! What's the game?

 *(***Koslowski*** *knocks him down)*

---

* *Quisling* the name of a Norwegian traitor who acted as advance agent for the German invasion of Norway in 1940; the name was then applied to any person of this kind who betrayed their own side.

Koslowski. Keepings down! Germans!

(More gun noise)

Hardy. Ey! Stop that shooting!. . . *(He stands up and shouts)*. . .
You'll kill somebody!

Koslowski. That is our work — killing Nazis.

Hardy. But there ain't no Germans.

Koslowski. What are these shooting at us, then? Boy Scouts? Is
paratroopers landed!. . . *(He shouts some foreign words. There
is more gun noise. Then* **Koslowski** *says)*. . . The Nazi fools are
shooting too high! Soon, we have them. One hand-grenade, and
. . . POOF!. . .

*(***Rudi*** appears. He is waving a piece of white cloth, tied to a twig.*
Koslowski *says)*

. . . Ah! See! Typical Nazis! Cowards, and improperly dressed,
too. I have a mind to shoot him as a spy!

Hardy. You can't shoot a man who's carrying a white flag. It's not fair.

Koslowski. Ah! The English gentleman! Always so ruddy fair! Perhaps
if your homes had been burnt to the ground you would not be so
concerned to be ruddy fair!

*(***The Poles*** grab ***Rudi*** and search him)*

Rudi. Rudi Golath. Sergeant. Luftwaffe 764532.

Koslowski. Spy! You will be shot, and all the others with you!

Rudi. There no others are. Back there, is children.

Hardy. CHILDREN?

Rudi. Ja. Six school kids.

Hardy. Is one called McGill?

Rudi. Ja. Chassy McGill.

Hardy. McGill. I might have known it!

Koslowski. Ah! These mad British!

(As **Koslowski** *shouts orders,* **The Polish Soldiers** *withdraw. Then,
there are the sounds of a police car driving up. Doors slam, and*
Liddell, Duty Officer Sanderson *and* **The Police Sergeant** *arrive.
There are more car noises, and* **Chas's Mum** *and* **Dad** *arrive.)*

Cem *(At the fortress)*. Are they all Quislings?

Chas. Look! There's my Mum and my Dad! Have they taken them
hostage? I can't shoot now.

Clogger. The Germans are going. Look! The police are coming! With your Mum and Dad!
Audrey. And Mr Liddell. . .
Nicky. And Rudi. Why didn't he go?
Chas. My Dad doesn't look scared. He looks. . . furious. . .
Cem. Oh, God, what have we done? Go away! Leave us alone!

*(***Clogger*** shoots, with* **Rudi***'s pistol.* **The Parents, The Home Guard** *and* **The Other Adults** *fall to the ground.)*

Chas *(Shouting).* Go back! Get out, or we'll shoot!. . . *(He screams).* . . Go away! Go away! Get lost, you rotten lot! Leave us alone!. . .

*(***Rudi*** gets up and walks slowly towards the fortress.* **Chas** *shrieks at him.)*

. . . Get back! Rudi, get back!
Cem. You're blocking our view! We'll fire! Get back!
Clogger. Oh, God!

(He fires, and **Rudi** *falls)*

Audrey *(Rushing forward and screaming).* Oh, Rudi!

*(***All the Children*** rush to him)*

Liddell *(Walking forward, and very much in command).* Clear the area! Clear the area! This is a military matter. That means you, Constable! And you, too, Sergeant!. . .

*(***Two Nurses*** approach, bringing a stretcher for* **Rudi***.* **Liddell** *calls to them)*

. . . Over here, Sister! Careful, now!

*(***The Children*** gather round. They are crying, touching, holding, and trying to help.)*

Nicky *(To* **Liddell***).* Can I go with him, Sir? Please. . .
Liddell. Very well. I'll see to you later. . .

*(***The Nurses*** take* **Rudi** *away, and* **Nicky** *follows. Then* **Liddell** *says to* **The Police***)*

. . . Now, Sergeant, you put this matter in my hands and I'm keeping it there for the moment. Your time will come. . .

(The Police stamp angrily away. Then **Liddell** *turns his attention to* **The Remaining Members of the Gang,** *saying)*

. . . Now! How about showing us. . . all this. . . McGill, will you?

(Then **The Adults** *and* **The Gang Members** *inspect the fortress. At first, all are very subdued. Then, admiration at the quality of the workmanship starts to show.)*

D.O. Sanderson *(Appreciatively).* This is a good 'ole. A very good 'ole indeed. I could 'ave done with this 'ole in the Somme in 1917! I'd like to take this whole thing over, Sar, for the 'Ome Guard. We 'aven't got nothing as good as this. . . *(He speaks to* **The Gang Members***).* . . Now, Lady and Gentlemen! Will you be so good as to hand over your weapons, please? We 'aven't got nothing as good as that machine-gun. . . .

*(***Clogger** *hands over* **Rudi***'s pistol.* **Chas** *lifts down the machine-gun, and* **All the Gang Members There** *place a hand on the barrel, as though swearing, again. Then* **Chas** *gives the gun to* **D.O. Sanderson,** *who says to* **Liddell***)*

. . . I dare say they can come up to the Post, sometimes, Sar, and see the guns?

*(***Liddell** *nods)*

Chas. Cem and I will come. And Audrey, if she's allowed. But Clogger and Nicky will have to go into a home.

Liddell. I'll do what I can to help to keep them together.

Chas. And can you get permission for us to write to Rudi if. . . If. . . And let us know how he gets on?

Liddell. I can certainly do that.

Dad *(From a distance).* How much longer are you going to hold those kids?

Liddell. I am acting under the authority of Northern Command, Sir. If you have any complaints, address them to the Brigadier, at York.

Mum. All I want is to get Chassy back home. He could have killed someone.

Dad *(Slowly).* I'll not say MUCH for my lad, except. . . He thought he was fighting the Germans.

D.O. Sanderson. Aye! That's one thing the kids didn't lack. GUTS!

SCENE 53

(The **McGill** *kitchen.* **Grand-da,** *in a chair, is asleep.* **Chas** *comes in, with* **Grand-da**'s *tin hat.)*

Chas *(Softly).* Grand-da! I borrowed your helmet. The one you wore at Caparetto. The one you used as a candle-stick, remember? You told me that was the original candle grease. . .

(As **Grand-da** *stirs, disturbed from his dreams of the First World War,* **Chas** *whispers to him)*

. . . Thanks. I don't need it any more.

selected titles
dramascripts